My Brother

by Geoff Patton
illustrated by David Clarke

to the school

to Sam's house

Con's house

2

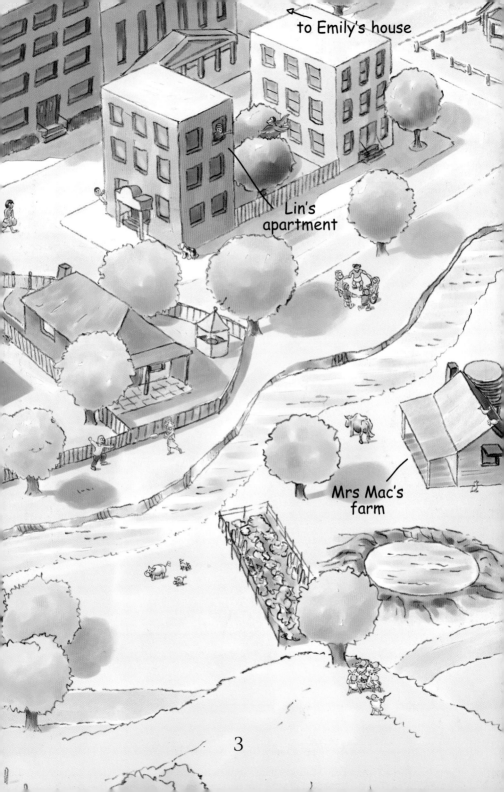

to Emily's house

Lin's apartment

Mrs Mac's farm

3

Hi. My name is Lin.
This is my family.

Mum

Tran,
my big brother

Chapter 1
Glow in the Dark

When my friends come over after school, I ask Mum, 'Can you tell Tran to stay away?'

But while we are playing popstars in my bedroom, Tran turns out the light. He puts on his glow-in-the-dark monster mask.

My friends **scream** and **scream**
and **scream**.

I say, 'Tran, take off your glow-in-the-dark
monster mask.' I say, 'Tran, you are in
big trouble.' I yell, 'Mum, Tran is in
big trouble!'

7

But Mum says, 'Sometimes big
brothers wear glow-in-the-dark
monster masks.'

I say, 'Sometimes I don't want
a big brother.'

Chapter 2
Too Many Peas

When we are eating dinner, I say to Mum, 'Can you tell Tran to stay away?'

But while I am talking to the cat, Tran slips his peas onto my plate.

I **scream** and **scream**
and **scream**.

I say, 'Tran, take off your peas.'
I say, 'Tran, you are in big trouble.'
I yell, 'Mum, Tran is in **big** trouble!'

But Mum says, 'Sometimes big brothers slip peas onto plates.'

I say, 'Sometimes I don't want a big brother.'

Chapter 3
The Missing Dolls

When I am playing with my bean bag dolls, I say to Mum, 'Can you tell Tran to stay away?'

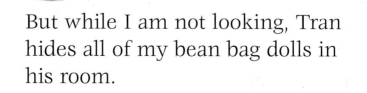

But while I am not looking, Tran hides all of my bean bag dolls in his room.

I **scream** and **scream** and **scream**.

Tran, you are in big trouble.

I say, 'Tran, give me back my bean bag dolls.' I say, 'Tran, you are in big trouble.' I yell, 'Mum, Tran is in **big** trouble!'

But Mum says, 'Sometimes big brothers hide bean bag dolls in their room.'

I say, 'Sometimes I don't want a big brother.'

Chapter 4

Lin Loves Josh

When I am drawing with my friend Josh, I say to Mum, 'Can you tell Tran to stay away?'

But while we are drawing big blue fish, Tran yells, 'Lin loves Josh.'

Josh **screams** and **screams** and **screams**.

I say, 'Tran, go away.' I say, 'Tran, you are in big trouble.' I yell, 'Mum, Tran is in **big** trouble!'

16

But Mum says, 'Sometimes big brothers say "Lin loves Josh"'.

I say, 'Sometimes I don't want a big brother.'

Chapter 5
A Big Fall

When I am riding my bike, I say
to Mum, 'Can you tell Tran to
stay away?'

But while I am riding, the little wheels
fall off the big wheel. I fall off too.

I **scream** and **scream**
and **scream**.

Tran says, 'I will take you inside.'
He says, 'Lin, you are in big trouble.'
He yells, 'Mum, Lin is in **big** trouble!'

He picks me up and helps me back inside.

Mum says, 'Sometimes it is good when big brothers don't stay away.'

I say, 'Sometimes I *do* want
a big brother.'

Survival Tips

1 Lock your bedroom door.

2 If he is in a bad mood, stay away.

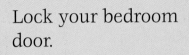

3 Tell him that you love him. Blow him a kiss in front of his friends, but make sure you can get away fast.

4 Lock your bedroom door.

5 If he takes your bean bag dolls, pretend you don't care. Then he will think he has wasted his time.

6 Lock your bedroom door.

Riddles and Jokes

Tran Did you hear about the boy who sat under a cow?

Lin He got a pat on the head.

Lin I would tell you a joke about my big brother and the pencil, but there is no point.

Lin My big brother is a real pain.

Mum It could be worse.

Lin How?

Mum He could be twins!

Lin Why did Tran jump up and down before taking his medicine?

Mum I don't know, why did Tran jump up and down before taking his medicine?

Tran Because it said, 'Shake well before using.'